Who's Been Eating My Porridge?

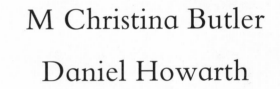

M Christina Butler

Daniel Howarth

LITTLE TIGER PRESS
London

Little Bear would not eat his porridge.

"All little bears eat porridge," Mummy said.
"It makes them big and strong."

But Little Bear shook his head. "No porridge,"
he said.

"Then I shall give it to Old Scary Bear
who lives in the wood," said Mummy.
     And Little Bear watched as Mummy Bear
took the porridge outside and left it on an
old tree stump.

That day, Little Bear climbed trees and
watched out for Old Scary Bear.

On the way home Daddy Bear said, "Did you see Scary Bear?"

"No," replied Little Bear, "because there *is* no Scary Bear!"

"Well, somebody has eaten your porridge," said Mummy Bear.

The next morning Daddy Bear put
some honey on Little Bear's porridge,
but Little Bear still would not eat it.

So Daddy Bear
took it outside
and left it on the
tree stump for
Old Scary Bear.

That day, Granny and Grandpa Bear
came to help pick berries.

"I hear you don't eat your porridge,"
said Grandpa. "It's no wonder there's
a Scary Bear about. Scary Bears
love porridge."

Little Bear ran over to the tree
stump and found that his porridge
bowl was empty again!

Next morning, Granny put some
honey and berries on Little Bear's
porridge. Little Bear held his nose
and closed his eyes. "No porridge!"
he cried. "I hate porridge!"

And so Grandpa took the porridge
outside again for Old Scary Bear.

That day, Little Bear's aunt and uncle and his two big cousins came to help gather nuts in the woods.

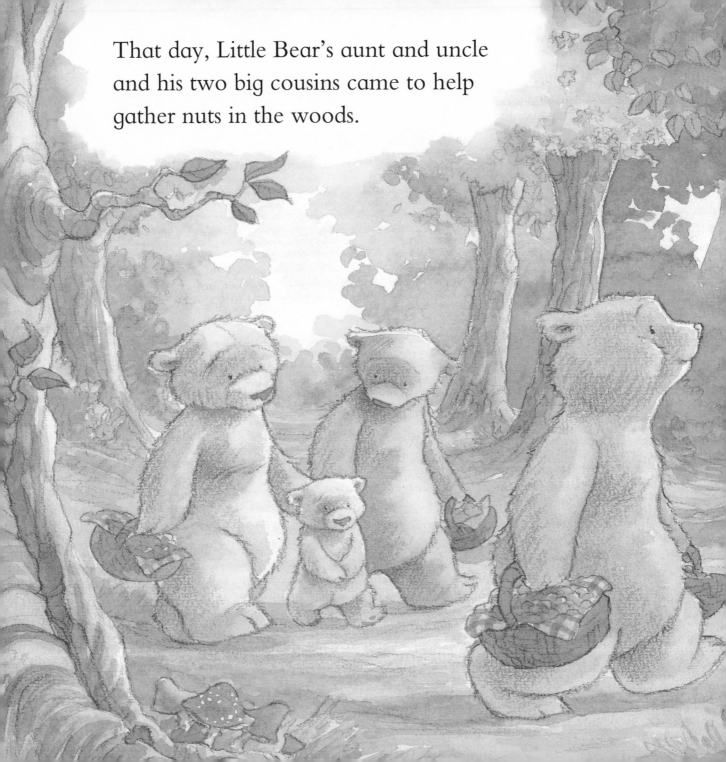

On the way home, Little Bear was very quiet and wouldn't speak to anyone.

"I expect he's tired," said Daddy Bear.

At supper time Little Bear wasn't feeling hungry. Daddy Bear took him upstairs and tucked him into bed.

That night Little Bear had a bad dream.
Old Scary Bear was chasing him through
the woods.

"I want your porridge," he growled.
"It makes me big and strong!"

Little Bear ran and ran with
his porridge … over the fields …
through the woods …
past the beehives …

until he came to the
old tree stump.

  "You're not having
my porridge!" he shouted
to Old Scary Bear, and he
ate up all his porridge ...
every bit.

And then he woke up.

The next morning at breakfast time,
Little Bear ate a bowl of porridge
with honey . . .

. . . and then he had
a second helping
with nuts and
berries.

All day Little Bear was very busy. He helped
Granny Bear and Mummy Bear make berries
into jam and put honey into jars.

Then he helped Grandpa Bear and
Daddy Bear who were storing the nuts.
    Suddenly Daddy said, "What's that noise?"
    All the bears peeked outside.

In front of the bear den were lots of little
animals all shouting, "Where's our porridge?
  "So *that's* who Old Scary Bear is!"
cried Little Bear with a giggle.

And from then on, Little Bear took
a bowl of porridge outside for
Old Scary Bear every morning.
And *he* always ate it!

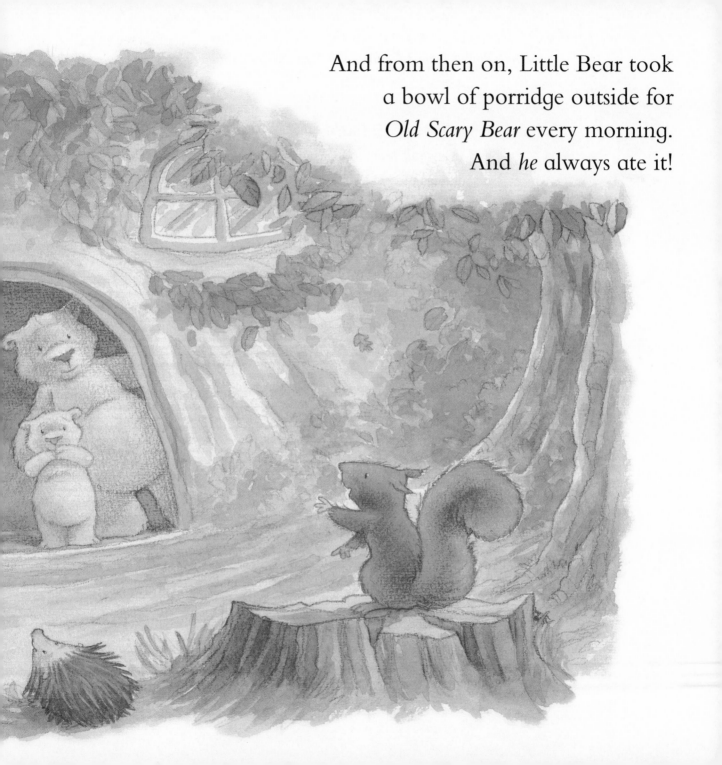

Especially for Daniel Cautley and Max Henry with love
~ M C B

To Mum and Dad, thank you
And to my little bears, who love their porridge
~ D H

LITTLE TIGER PRESS
1 The Coda Centre, 189 Munster Road,
London SW6 6AW
www.littletigerpress.com

First published in Great Britain 2004
This edition published 2012

Text copyright © M Christina Butler 2004
Illustrations copyright © Daniel Howarth 2004
M Christina Butler and Daniel Howarth have
asserted their rights to be identified as the author
and illustrator of this work under the Copyright,
Designs and Patents Act, 1988